Dance the Hora, Isadora!

written by Gloria Koster • illustrated by Barbara Bongini

APPLES & HONEY PRESS

To Eric, my forever partner in dance and everything else.
—G.K.

*To the sweetest and strongest woman of my life:
my mother, Alessandra.*
—B.B.

Apples & Honey Press
An Imprint of Behrman House Publishers
Millburn, New Jersey 07041
www.applesandhoneypress.com

ISBN 978-1-68115-587-6

Library of Congress Cataloging-in-Publication Data
Names: Koster, Gloria, author. | Bongini, Barbara, illustrator.
Title: Dance the Hora, Isadora! / by Gloria Koster ; illustrated by Barbara Bongini.
Description: Millburn, New Jersey : Apples & Honey Press, [2022] | Summary:
"A girl learns to dance the Hora at her cousin's wedding, then brings
her new moves to dance class"-- Provided by publisher.
Identifiers: LCCN 2021042513 | ISBN 9781681155876 (hardcover)
Subjects: CYAC: Folk dancing--Fiction. | Weddings--Fiction. |
Jews--Fiction. | LCGFT: Picture books.
Classification: LCC PZ7.K8528 Dan 2022 | DDC [E]--dc23
LC record available at https://lccn.loc.gov/2021042513

The illustrations in this book were made on a computer with a graphic pen.
The artist used pastel textures to enrich the clothing and other details.

Design by Elynn Cohen
Edited by Alef Davis
Printed in China

9 8 7 6 5 4 3 2 1

0922/B1898/A4

I love Monday afternoons. At ballet class
I practice my pirouettes, pliés, glissades,
and jetés.

Every week when class is almost over, Madame
Delphine gives us time to show off any dance we
choose. She asks, "Who'd like to go first?"

Lucy likes hip-hop. Her boom-boom music rattles the walls as she tumbles, twists, and does fancy splits.

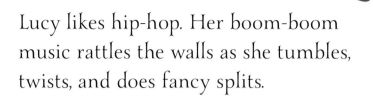

Mateo takes ballroom lessons. He knows how to tango and can cha-cha-cha.

Chloe is our step-dance star. Tap-tap go her toes. Up go her knees, reaching almost as high as her chin.

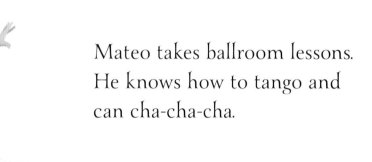

When Chloe finished her routine last week, I felt Madame's eyes on me. "Isadora, would you like a turn?" she asked.

More than anything, I wanted to say yes, but I had nothing to share. If only I could shine like Lucy, Mateo, and Chloe.

On the way home, Grandma
could see I needed some cheering up.
"Why such a sad face?" she asked.

"Everyone in class has a special dance," I said.
"Everyone except me!"

"I have a feeling you may find one very soon," Grandma said,
"maybe even this weekend."

I knew she was thinking about the wedding.
On Sunday, Cousin Rachel was getting married
to Adam.

Do you know who the flower girl was? . . . *MOI*
(that's French for ME)!

I would be the first one to walk down the aisle. We were
getting ready on the wedding day when Rachel said,
"I need my little cousin with me to calm my nerves."
Obviously, I had a very important job!

Standing under the chuppah, I watched the rabbi bless the bride and groom. I had the best view when they said, "I do," but my favorite part came at the end. Adam lifted his foot and stomped on a glass! *SMAAASH!*

After the ceremony, it was time to party. "Listen, Isadora," Grandma said. "The band is starting!"

I heard a tune deep and slow and a singer's voice clear and low. *Hava na-gila, hava na-gila.*

Adam's groomsmen stood shoulder to shoulder, swaying. Rachel's bridesmaids flicked off their high heels. Guests rushed onto the dance floor for the hora.

They formed a circle.
Like a giant wheel, it began to turn.

Dancers skipping, jumping, whirling, kicking.
My feet tingled, but did I dare join in?

In the end Grandma decided for me. She took my hand and found a place for us in the circle.

"We'll practice the steps later," she said. "For now, just let the joy sweep you along."

I held on tight to keep from tripping.
The floor pounded.
The music got louder and faster.
Party dresses swirled as we went round and round.
My feet were flying!

Soon the large circle broke apart. A line snaked around the room. That's when Grandma took me aside for the real lesson.

She raised her skirt above her knees so I could copy every step, kick, and hop.

"You look like a pro," she said.

"Let's keep going," I begged. But Grandma was fanning
her face.

"I need to catch my breath, honey," she said. "Besides, we
don't want to miss what's happening next. Look!"

People had gathered around the bride and groom.
Seated on chairs, Rachel and Adam were lifted high,
then higher, so high that I was afraid they'd tip over.

As soon as they landed safely, the music stopped.
"No more hora?" I asked.

"We'll dance again later," Grandma promised.
"Right now it's time to eat."

On the way to our table I overheard someone say,
"I wish I could move as gracefully as that girl!" I felt
so proud. All that dancing had made me hungry too,
and dinner was delicious.

When the meal was over, Rachel made an announcement.
"We need a special someone to help cut the cake."

Do you know who that special someone was? ... *MOI!*

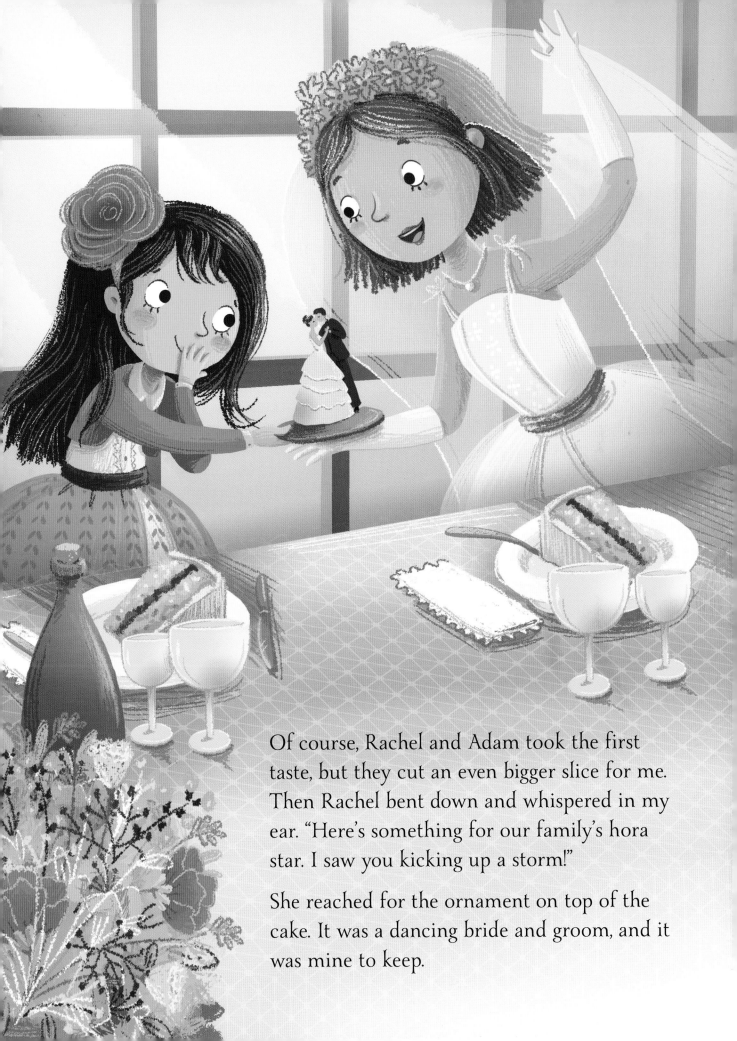

Of course, Rachel and Adam took the first taste, but they cut an even bigger slice for me. Then Rachel bent down and whispered in my ear. "Here's something for our family's hora star. I saw you kicking up a storm!"

She reached for the ornament on top of the cake. It was a dancing bride and groom, and it was mine to keep.

On Monday afternoon, I couldn't wait to show my new dance to the class.

First we practiced our pirouettes,
pliés,
glissades,
and jetés.

Then I asked Madame to add "Hava Nagila" to her playlist.

"Class, come watch Isadora dance the hora."

My heart fluttered, but as soon as
the music started, my legs took over.

I skipped, jumped, whirled, and kicked all around the room,
remembering everything Grandma had taught me.

The joy swept me along, and I invited my friends to come and learn the steps.

Lucy was first, followed by Mateo and Chloe. Soon the entire class was part of my circle—even Madame Delphine.

"MAGNIFIQUE!" she said when the music came to an end.

"Thank you so much, Isadora! Now we all can dance the hora!"

A Note for Families

We all have our own ways to shine. When we follow our passions, we can feel joy and bring light into the world. Isadora is happiest when she's dancing. Do you have an activity that makes you especially happy? Is there a friend or a grown-up who encourages you to follow your passion?

Isadora shines when her grandmother teaches her the hora, a lesson that includes the dance steps and something even more meaningful. When Grandma takes Isadora's hand and leads her to the circle, she is demonstrating the Jewish value of *l'dor vador*, "from generation to generation." When we pass our beautiful Jewish traditions from generation to generation, we can deepen connections to our loved ones and our communities.

If you've ever gone to a Jewish celebration, you've probably experienced the magic of the hora. Nothing brings people together more quickly than the opening notes of "Hava Nagila," the song that usually accompanies the dance. The hora, which began long ago in Southeastern Europe, has become a favorite in Israel and among Jewish people everywhere. Joining hands for the hora can fill us with a sense of unity and freedom. And you don't have to be Jewish to dance the hora. Everyone is welcome!